FRANCESCA CAVALLO

THE LONG JUMP

THE STORY OF JEAN-BAPTISTE ALAIZE

Illustrated by **Kezna Dalz**

undercats

EDITORIAL DIRECTOR: Francesca Cavallo
STORY: Francesca Cavallo
ILLUSTRATIONS: Kezna Dalz
GRAPHIC DESIGNER: Francesca Pignataro
Francesca Cavallo's portrait © Camilla Mandarino
Kezna Dalz's portrait © Joana Dahloff

The Long Jump: The Story of Jean-Baptiste Alaize is published by
Undercats, Inc. We are a small, independent publisher with a big
mission: to radically increase diversity in children's media and inspire
families to take action for equality.

To see more of our books and download bonus materials and free
stories, come visit us at www.undercats.com.

Printed in Canada

At Undercats, we do our best every day to minimize our carbon
footprint. We printed this book using FSC® certified materials only,
and we always make sure to print at plants that are close to our
distribution centers to reduce carbon emissions due to transportation.

Dear Reader,

When I was a kid, growing up in South Carolina, I loved reading books. But none of the books I read told my story, and none of the characters looked like me: a Black girl with a disability. Even now that I'm grown up, I still have to look really hard to find disabled characters in books being published. Which is why it's so great to see books like the one you're reading today! It's so important that disabled children no longer feel unseen in the pages they read.

This book about Jean-Baptiste Alaize's life is one that discusses many realities that exist in our world - surviving a war, transracial adoption, living with a disability, finding a purpose, and achieving one's dreams.

Jean-Baptiste's story struck a chord in my heart: here was a Black disabled child, just like me, finding their way in a world that never considered them. Like Jean-Baptiste, it was only with the amazing support and love from my family that I have been able to fulfill my dreams.

Stories about Black disabled people deserve to be told and read by everyone. This book is a part of the push to get more diverse disability stories onto every child's bookshelf, so that no one has to grow up without seeing kids that look like they do in the books they love.

Vilissa Thompson, LMSW
Founder of Ramp Your Voice!, LLC
Social Worker, Speaker, Writer, Activist,
and Maker of Good Trouble

To the children who survive wars.
May we find the courage
to listen.

ONCE UPON A TIME,

in the tiny African country of Burundi, a little boy called Mouguicha was playing with his friends in a beautiful field surrounded by banana plantations.

"Pass the ball!" a boy shouted,
but Mouguicha didn't hear.

He was distracted by a group of men nearby.
They looked angry, and were shouting.
"Who are they?" he asked.

"Never mind them. Just pass the ball,"
his friend said, and they got on with their game.

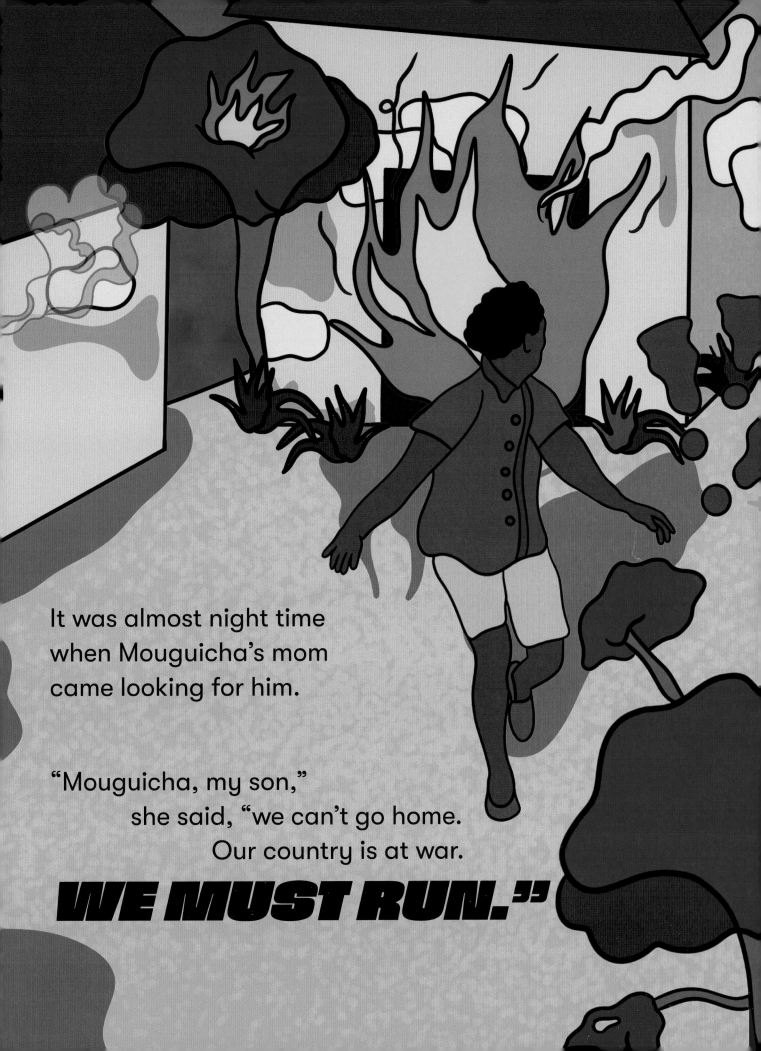

It was almost night time
when Mouguicha's mom
came looking for him.

"Mouguicha, my son,"
        she said, "we can't go home.
            Our country is at war.

WE MUST RUN."

She picked him up in her arms and started to run.
But the angry men caught them.

They killed Mouguicha's mom and they thought
they had killed the little boy too.

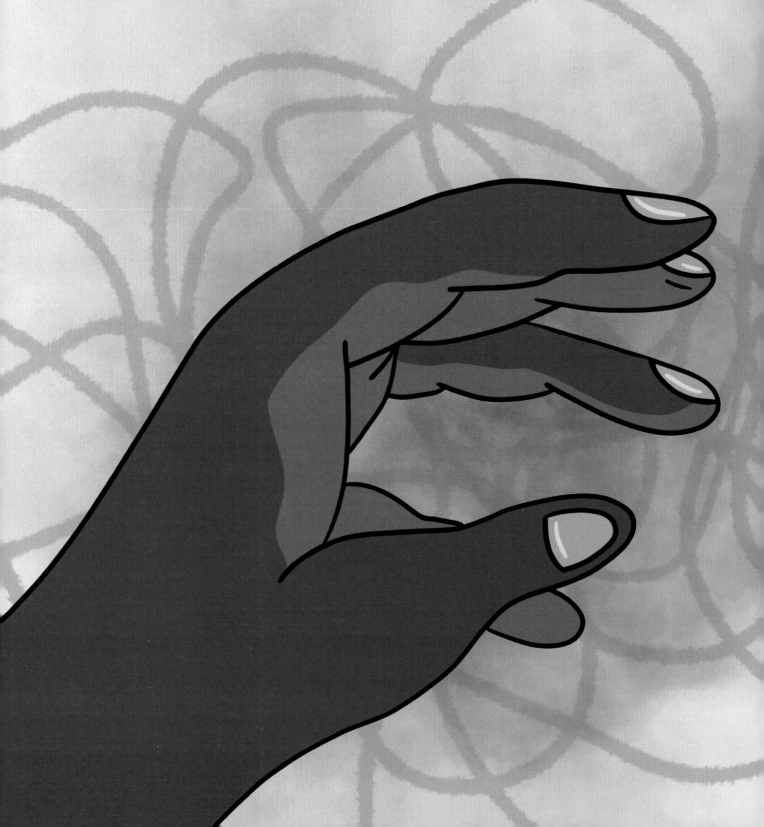

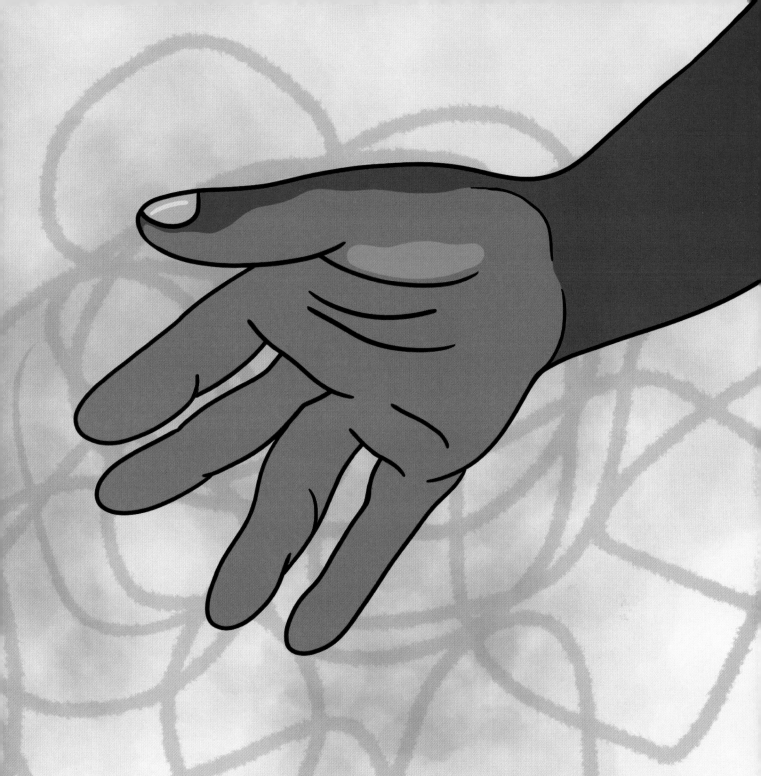

They were wrong.
Mouguicha was badly injured, but

When he woke up, Mouguicha found himself
in the hospital. To save his life,
the doctors had amputated one of his legs.

Mouguicha was sad because he missed his mom,
but he was also grateful because he still had
one leg to move around on and play like he used to.

When Mouguicha recovered fully from his surgery, he went to live in an orphanage with many other children who did not have parents.

It wasn't long before he was playing soccer with his new friends.

One day,
a man showed up
at the orphanage.

His skin was so pale!
Mouguicha had never seen
anyone like him before.

The man introduced himself in French,
because he didn't speak Kirundi:
"Je suis Robert," he said.

But Mouguicha did not understand
because he didn't speak French.

They did have one thing in common though:
the tall, white, French man and the little, Black,
Burundian boy both used

CRUTCHES.

Robert had lost his right leg
in an accident years before.

For a few days, Robert and Mouguicha
played together at the orphanage,
getting to know each other.

But every evening, they heard shots
being fired all around and they were scared.
The war wasn't over.

Robert adopted Mouguicha as his son and they flew back together to France.

When they arrived in France, Mouguicha met his adoptive mom, Danielle, and his adoptive brother, Julian.

'Mouguicha' means *blessed and lucky child.*

But back then, not many white people understood the beauty of African names. So Mouguicha was given a French name:

Jean-Baptiste.

His new name wasn't the only thing
he had to get used to.
The town where he now lived
was completely different
from his village
in Burundi.

The trees and the houses looked different,
but above all, the people looked really

DIFFERENT.

In Burundi, everyone was Black.
But here?
Everyone was white.

Jean-Baptiste and his brother were
the only two Black children in town.

When he was 8 years old,
Jean-Baptiste got a very exciting present:
a prosthetic leg!

He loved his new leg,
but he was afraid
that if the other children knew about it,
they would tease him.

So he decided to keep it a secret.
He always wore shoes and long pants everywhere.

At school, he loved to run.

Soon, he was not just running in races but

WINNING!

One day, he decided to show his PE teacher his special leg. The teacher was amazed.

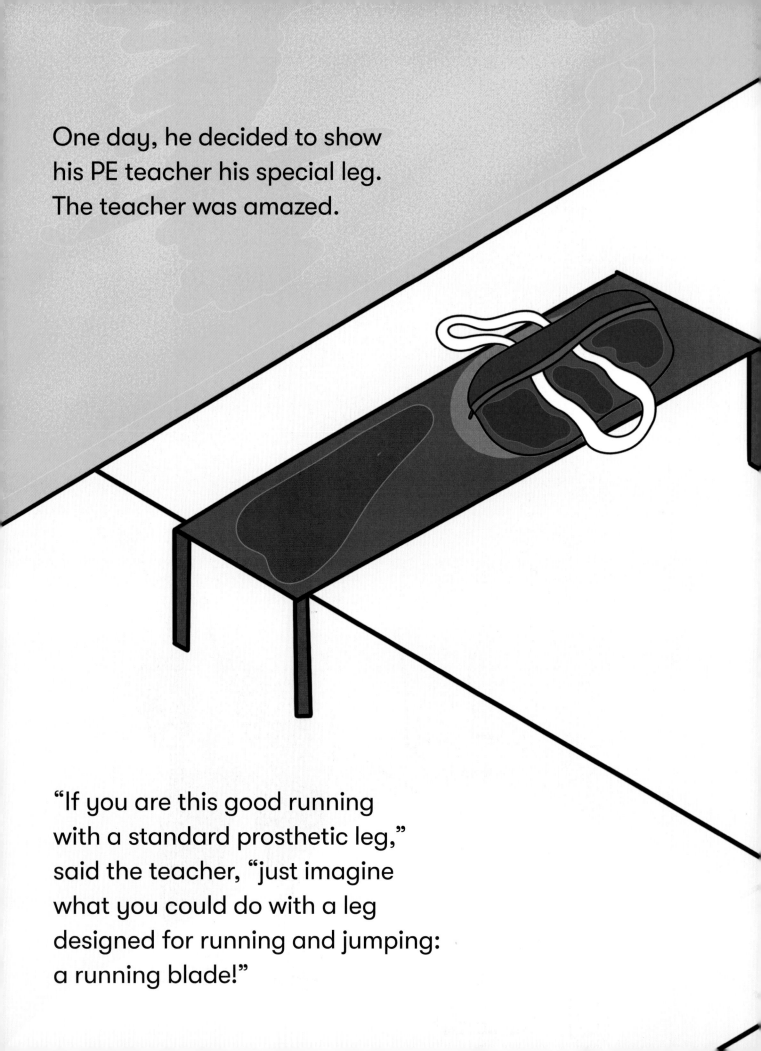

"If you are this good running with a standard prosthetic leg," said the teacher, "just imagine what you could do with a leg designed for running and jumping: a running blade!"

"How much does that cost?"
asked Jean-Baptiste
with a worried look on his face.

The running blade was $17,000.
It was way more than
Jean-Baptiste's family
could afford.

What can I do?
thought Jean-Baptiste.

Jean-Baptiste asked his dad.
And his dad asked their friends.
And their friends asked everyone
they knew to help.

Soon they had raised enough money to buy Jean-Baptiste a beautiful, new running blade.

When Jean-Baptiste ran,
he felt free.
When he jumped,
he felt like he was

FLYING.

With his new running blade, there was
no stopping him. By the time he was 23,
he had won four long-jump world championships.

When he was 26, he won a bronze medal
at the London Paralympic Games!

When he felt ready,
Jean-Baptiste flew back to Burundi.
The war was finally over.

He hugged his sisters,
and forgave the men
who had killed his mother.

"I do not have
any more hate."
said Mouguicha,
the lucky and blessed
man who flew higher
than anyone.

MY LONG JUMPS

What makes you feel like you're flying?

JEAN-BAPTISTE ALAIZE

Jean-Baptiste Alaize was born in Burundi in 1991, during the civil war between the Hutus and Tutsis. When he was three years old, his village was attacked. His mother was killed but he survived. His right tibia had to be amputated to save his life.

In 1998, Jean-Baptiste was adopted by a French family and he moved to Montelimar, France. In 2005, he got a prosthetic leg and proved himself a gifted athlete. He especially loved sprinting and long jump. Jean-Baptiste went on to break world records. He became a two-time Paralympian and won a bronze medal at the London 2017 Para Athletics Championship.

In 2010, he joined France's National Institute of Sport, Expertise, and Performance (INSEP). He became an Ambassador for Peace with an organization called 'Peace and Sports', and helped set up their Friendship Games – bringing together young people from the countries around Africa's Great Lakes to build friendship and peace through sports.

Jean-Baptiste stars in the documentary *Rising Phoenix* (2020).

Learn more at
www.jbalaize.com

FRANCESCA CAVALLO is an award-winning, New York Times bestselling author, entrepreneur and activist. She co-created the *Good Night Stories for Rebel Girls* book series and podcast, and was the recipient of the *Publishers Weekly* StarWatch Award in 2018. In 2019, she parted ways with Rebel Girls - which she had co-founded - to start Undercats, Inc. Francesca's work has been translated into more than 50 languages, and her books have sold more than 5 million copies worldwide.

Instagram: @francescatherebel

KEZNA DALZ / Teenadult is a multidisciplinary artist from Montreal, Canada. The recurring themes of her work are feminism, the fight against racism, and issues to do with popular culture and sexuality. She loves to make difficult subjects accessible using her own distinctive style. She works with bold shapes, strong outlines and bright colors to create eye-catching designs and powerful artwork.

Instagram: @teenadultt

Undercats is a small, independent publisher with a big mission:
to radically increase diversity in children's media and inspire families around the world
to take action for equality. We are a female led, LGBTQ+ owned company
with a very diverse team spread across two continents.

For us, books are opportunities to create human connections. We'd love to connect with you,
which is why we created our newsletter. Sign up if you would like to receive occasional,
upfliting updates about our upcoming projects.

www.undercats.com/newsletter

Let us know what you think about this book!

Instagram: @undercatsmedia Twitter: @undercatsmedia

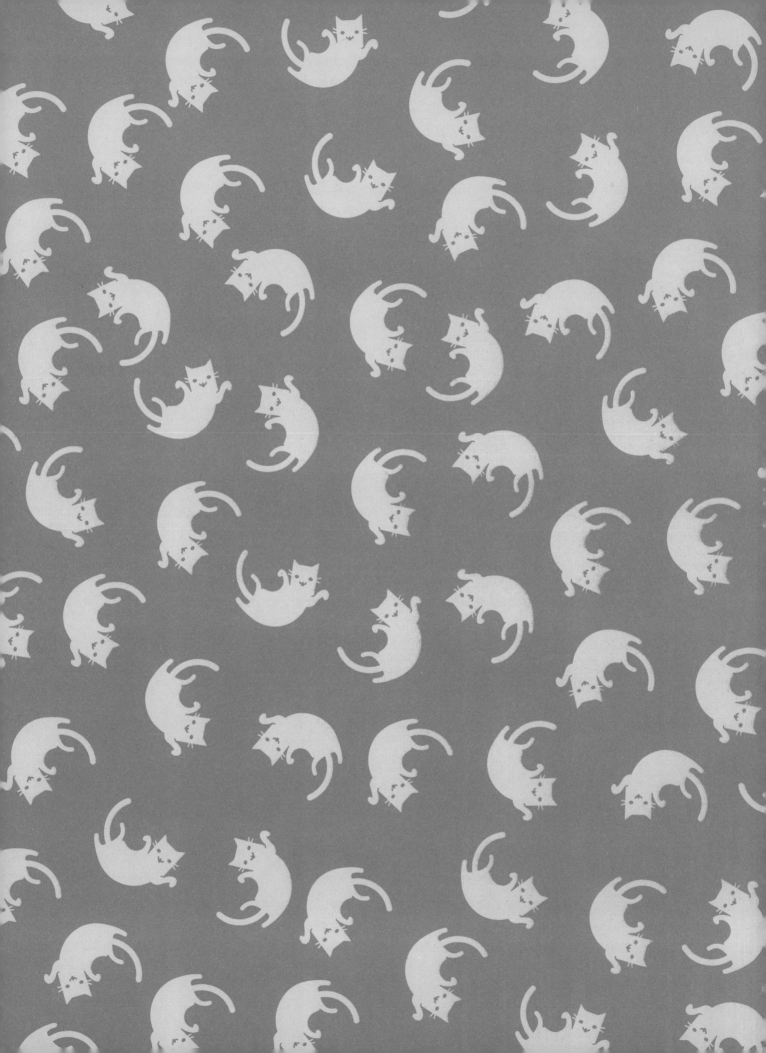